Calling ALL CaRS

written by
Sue Fliess

illustrated by
Sarah Beise

sourcebooks
jabberwocky

Published by Sourcebooks Jabberwocky, an imprint of Sourcebooks, Inc.
P.O. Box 4410, Naperville, Illinois 60567-4410
(630) 961-3900
Fax: (630) 961-2168
www.sourcebooks.com

Library of Congress Cataloging-in-Publication data is on file with the publisher.
Source of Production: Leo Paper, Heshan City, Guangdong Province, China
Date of Production: December 2015
Run Number: 5005137

Printed and bound in China.
LEO 10 9 8 7 6 5 4 3 2 1

For my Madsters and Little "A"
—Sarah

For Kevin, thanks for being my
road trip partner for life
—Sue

Beach cars,
town cars,

tops-go-down cars.

Zip through tunnels.
Make no stops.

Climb up over mountaintops.

Long cars,
WIDE cars,

who's inside
cars?

Smash cars,
ram cars,

traffic jam
cars.

**Yellow taxis,
limousines,**

cars that carry kings and queens.

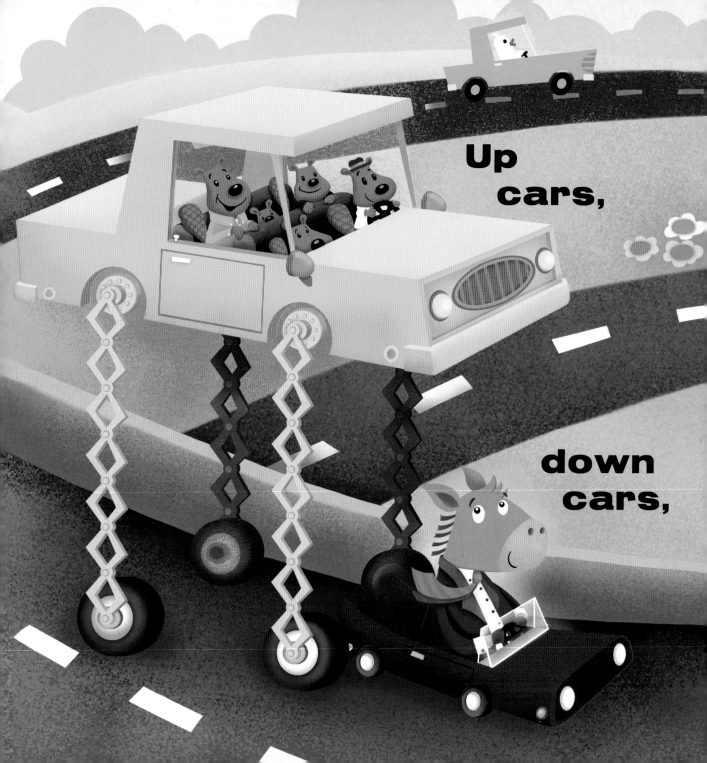

circus-clown
cars

Fast cars,

slow cars,

way-down-low cars.

HONK!

HONK!

Honking horns and changing lanes.

Ice and snow?
Let's put on chains!

Trip cars,

track cars,

dogs-in-back cars.

Love cars,  **hug cars,**

rainbow-bug cars.

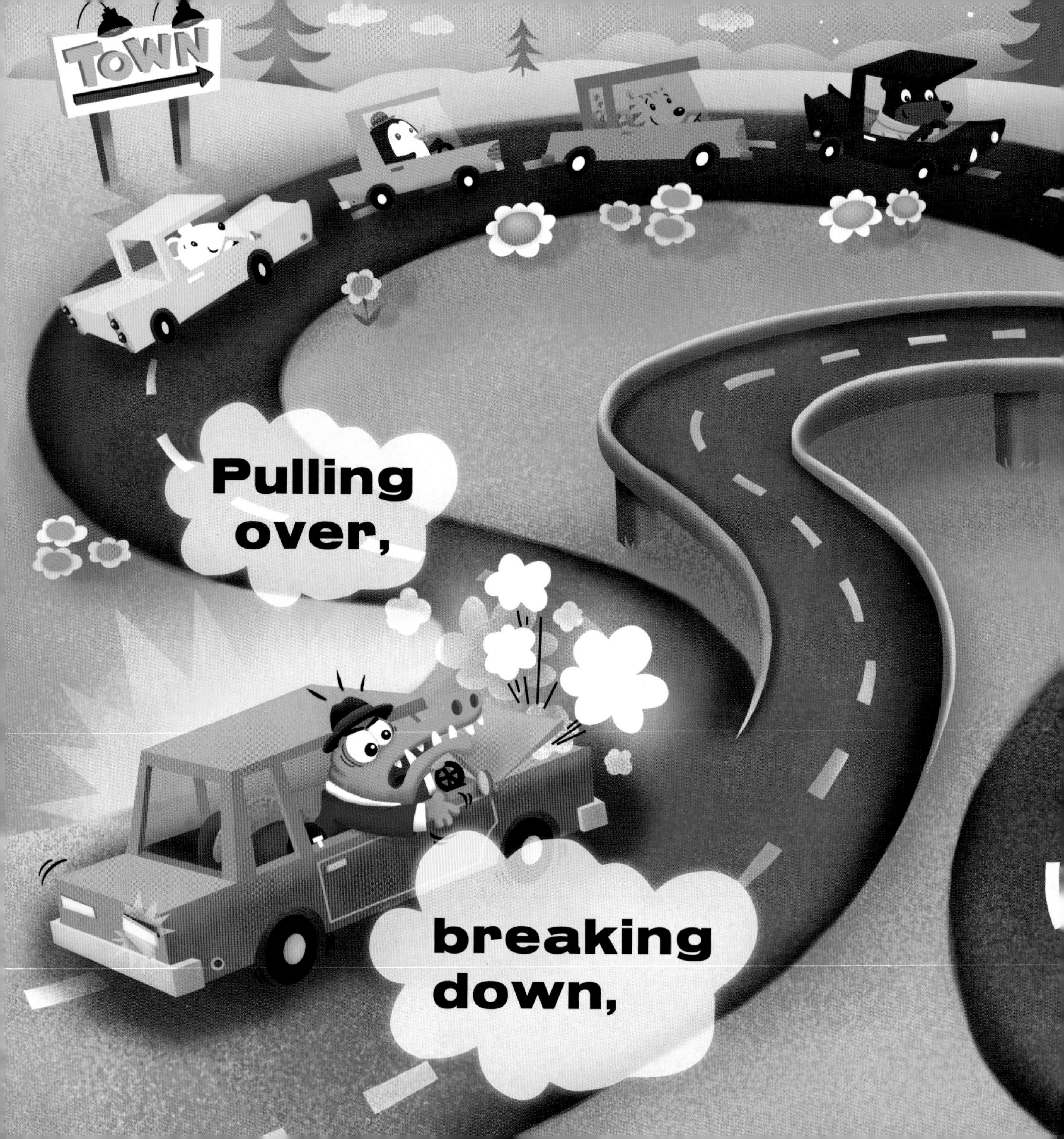

Pulling
over,

breaking
down,

need a tow

back
into town.

**Old cars,
new cars,**

starry-view cars.

Rest, cars.

Hush, cars.

No more
rush, cars.

Cars pull in, turn off the light.

Sweet dreams,
sleepy cars...

good night!